A.E. Hefny is an American-Egyptian who has been passionate about writing since fifth grade. His interest in different genres has led him to try his hand at several kinds of stories, sometimes even crossing them together. *Where One Ends, the Other Begins* is a cultivation of such passion and interests.

H.G. Wells

Oscar Mentenier

A.E. Hefny

Where One Ends, The Other Begins

Austin Macauley Publishers™
London • Cambridge • New York • Sharjah

This is a work of fiction. Names, characters, businesses, places, events, locales, and incidents are either the products of the author's imagination or used in a fictitious manner. Any resemblance to actual persons, living or dead, or actual events is purely coincidental.

A CIP catalogue record for this title is available from the British Library.

ISBN 9781398475762 (Paperback)
ISBN 9781398476967 (ePub e-book)

www.austinmacauley.com

First Published 2023
Austin Macauley Publishers Ltd®
1 Canada Square
Canary Wharf
London
E14 5AA

Chapter 1

The White Horse is often short on visitors these days, much to the mischarging of Mr and Mrs Thompson's. Isaac has already come knocking to "Send his regards," and is now sitting in the corner, waiting for his order of eggs and bacon, just to rub it all in.

So, it was quite a shock when a visitor, a stranger no less, set foot into their inn, tiredly waving as the wind took a few snipes at him before he closed the door.

"Hello," he said in a low tone, thumping his luggage, a great black bag, on the ground.

"Come in, son," said Mr Thompson, distinguishing the man's age from his soft, but clear voice. "You must be exhausted."

"Oh, you have no idea," said the visitor with a smile.

He was a youngster, his features fresh and clean-shaven. His hair was cramped from having resided in his hat for the last few hours, and though he kept a calm composure, Isaac's sharp eyes could spot his arms and legs shivering.

"Give this boy a room, will you, Derrick?" said Isaac, slowly sipping his drink. "He's clearly been walking."

"We know how to do our job, Isaac," said Florence Thompson, key in hand. "And we suggest you finish your meal. Weather like this doesn't pick sides, as I'm sure you know." He evaded her glare and minded his own business afterwards. "Jenny! Take his luggage! This is the best we could get." She said to her husband as he took the key, studied the room number, and nodded to her in agreement. Jenny came from the back, shyly smiling at their guest as she went for his bag.

"Oh, that wouldn't be necessary," he said lightly.

"It's quite heavy, you see."

"That what I pay Jenny for," said Derrick decisively. "Right this way." They went two floors up till they reached to Room 44. "Here we are, sir. The finest room in the inn."

It was small, but designed with enough care and space that one could at the very least manoeuvre through it without much difficulty. The bed, toilet, two chairs, and desk were all set in place, with a fireplace to accommodate the experience. The walls were covered in light blue, the rug was warm, the wooden floor was smooth with only tiny creaks leaking through, and on one picture, that of a daily activity at the harbour, hung over the desk.

"I never met anyone who enjoyed the harbour," said the visitor, watching it before getting bored and staring out the window.

"Well, when everyone and their mother smells like fish and rat shit, it's hard to get sentimental about it, sir," said Derrick before being nudged by Jenny as she lit the fireplace. "Apologies, sir. Jenny, get his plate ready."

She uttered a faint "Yes, sir," before leaving. The stranger kept watching the snowfall. "Something on your mind, sir?"

"No," said the young man, adjusting his glasses. "Just contemplating my surroundings."

Already? thought Derrick. "Well, I hope they are comfortable."

"May I smoke a pipe in here?"

"Certainly, sir."

"I appreciate your hospitality. Please send Mrs Thompson my regards."

"Well, hospitability is our job, but a compliment doesn't hurt. I'll tell her that." He heard Jenny's oncoming footsteps and moved out of the doorway to let her pass.

"Your dinner, sir," said Jenny as she placed a furnished silver tray on the desk.

"Thank you," he quietly said, the calm smile edging on his lips. She nodded in reply and left.

"One last thing," said Derrick. "May I know your name?"

"Certainly. Oliver Dawkins."

"That will be all, then. Good night, sir."

"Good night." As soon as he left, Dawkins slumped in the chair and started munching.

By the time Derrick had come down, Isaac had left, and the lights were out. Florence was already placing the last chair upside down.

"Come on," she said, motioning him, "The weather will be quiet tomorrow."

"Sure."

"How is he?"

"Don't know. Sends his regards, though."

"Must be a gentleman, then." They dressed for the night and tugged inside their sheets without much of a care for anything.

Chapter 2

The next day, Florence came to pick the stranger's tray, which he left outside. Kneeling to pick it up, the door knob turned and he popped his head outside.

"Ah, good morning, Mrs Thompson!" he announced, sending her yelping backwards. He was dressed in his pyjamas, his hair scattered about, with specks of water on his glasses.

"Good morning, sir," said Florence, catching her breath. "Did you sleep well?"

"Yes, it was just what I needed! Thank you for your hospitality."

"Yes, my husband already said that. Would you mind if I fix your bed, sir?"

"Of course!" He stepped aside and lit a pipe as she went on her business.

"I should let you know, Mrs Thompson, that around 3:00, I'll have the rest of my luggage delivered. I've already sent them the address, so they know their destination."

"I see. Tell me, sir, what are you doing here in West Sussex?"

"You and your husband are quite straightforward, aren't you?" he said with a laugh.

"Guests are still strangers, Mr Dawkins. We care for our business's reputation."

"I suppose." She heard the sound of silver being struck, and looked up to see a piece of shilling strike his palm. The same unassuming smile was still plastered on his face. "See this?" He held it to her, showing the head. "This is my father's will."

"I'm sorry for your loss, sir."

"Oh, he's not dead, he just gave me this to teach me a lesson. You see, this luggage has all my needs; clothes, notes, and this coin. The rest, he told me, is to be won by my own hand. I am an adult, he said, and it's time I act like one. So here I am." He flopped on the bed like an energetic child, dampening it. "What about you, Mrs Thompson? Do you have children?"

"No," she said in appalled finality, warning him not to continue the subject. His cheerful exterior didn't indicate whether he got the message or lost interest in the subject.

"Do you often have strangers coming in? The town seems awfully small."

"Aye, it is," said Florence, checking the time. "I will warn you first hand, sir, this is a nice place, but the neighbours will gossip."

"What do you advice, then?"

"I'd say keep your mind off of it. Greet us as you would anyone else."

"No exaggerations, then? I appreciate it, Mrs Thompson. I can't stand flashiness. It reminds me of a job interview."

"That makes two of us, Mr Dawkins." Her handiwork finally over, she turned to him. "Now, then, shall we see you for breakfast?" He flipped the coin once more.

"Certainly! If I may have some of that egg and bacon once more, I would be delighted!"

"As you wish." She excused herself and checked on Jenny, who was sweeping the third floor. "Jenny, are they all set?"

"Mr Cartwright is still asleep, Ma'am," said Jenny.

Nodding, she went about her business, setting up the plate for their guest. After he was done, he called it a day and left the house. Satisfied, Florence went down, empty plate in hand, to find the inn populated with the usual faces she had memorized for over ten years. Some aged, and some still looked the same, all of them having their daily morning gathering before going back to their routine. They would sit down, individually or in groups, talking about politics, the oddities of last night, and confessions. Today, as expected, they were all whispering about one subject in particular.

Her husband was serving breakfast to Ms Huston, who was having her traditional plate of fish and chips along with black tea before opening her sweet shop.

"Ah, Florence!" she exclaimed, waving at her. "How are you, dear?!"

"Oh, you know, business as usual. Quite a weather, huh?"

"A bother, an absolute bother! Why, the wind cracked my window so hard, I had to throw it away and get Simon to repair it." She waved at a younger, brown haired man, who saluted her with the tip of his hat in return before returning to his mates.

"Oh, that's terrible!" said Florence as Ms Huston briefly blushed.

"Yes, yes! Now, then, Derrick has been evasive again."

He heard them lower their voices and sensed their heads turning to his direction.

"Dear, remember what we agreed on?" He shrugged his shoulders as he went behind the counter.

"She asked about the boy."

"Oh, that Dawkins fellow..." Florence looked around, but couldn't find him.

"He left," her husband confirmed. "Finished his plate and was on his way."

"He was quite—voracious," said Ms Huston, having her first sip, "And—well, it's not my place to judge, but he's not exactly untidy—frankly, his cramped hair aside, he would strike me as handsome, but he's a little, well—not eccentric, but unfocused. Derrick wouldn't tell me anything about him, other than his name."

"For God's sake, Emily, it was midnight, and we were off to bed," said Derrick, fixing another meal for Johnathon and George, the local undertakers. "Didn't he tell you anything?" he asked Florence. She shook her head.

"But still, to arrive at such an hour," said George, stroking his chin, "In this weather, and here of all places. It's quite peculiar, don't you think?"

"Come now," said Johnathon, "Just because we're small doesn't mean we don't exist."

"He's a blunt fellow," said Florence, "Speaks his mind, but he seems harmless. To be frank, he's quite naive. Told me his father didn't leave him anything except for some belongings that he had to make his way through the world."

"Must be a rich bloke," said Mrs Archer, the owner of the local bakery, "To toss his son to the wolves like that."

"Well, there you have it," said Derrick, wiping his forehead, "A boy on a pilgrimage. Nothing special."

"What's his name again?" asked George.

"Oliver Dawkins," answered Isaac as he made his entrance. "Good morning, everyone." They all responded, even a reluctant Florence, except for Derrick, who was glaring at him. The guest merely replied with a smile.

"The usual?" asked Florence in monotone.

"Yes, please. Now, as you may know," he said, addressing the audience, "This fellow, Dawkins, is new around here. With that said, I would propose as mayor of this town that we treat him as if he existed yesteryear. After all, we could use a boost every now and then, correct?"

"You met him?" asked Dr Houseman, the town's local doctor.

"I shook hands with him. He seems like a pleasant fellow, even if a little too chipper for my taste. Said he was simply walking around town, getting used to the scenery. Oh yes, he's got equipment coming around this afternoon at your doorstep, Thompson."

"Yes, I'm quite aware of that," replied Florence. He chose to ignore her.

"Did he say what kind of luggage?" inquired Houseman.

"Seems you have competition, doctor. The fellow's a graduate of surgery from the Medical School of Oxford, and those are his tools." Excited murmurs echoed around the room, with even Jenny in the corner gasping in surprise. "Therefore," announced Isaac, "I have decided to invite him to tomorrow's gathering, and have him mingle with us. I'm sorry I wasn't being democratic in such matter, but I hope you don't mind." He was ignored in light of other mumbles and buzzes. Isaac pursed his lips before grabbing his hat. "Well then..."

"Isaac," said Florence, "Your plate."

"Oh, right, right!" He awkwardly stumbled to an empty seat and took his place. She placed it and his tea in front of it. "Thank you, Florence," he nodded and smiled at her, well aware that Derrick was eyeing him.

He proceeded to focus on the taste of coffee pouring down his chest, causing him slight coughs before controlling himself with some deep breathing.

After paying the tab, he gave farewells to those who still remained and swung through the door. A few minutes passed, and eventually, everyone was gone.

"Did he say anything else?" asked Derrick as he swept the tables.

"He asked if we had children, I said no," said Florence plainly, wiping a cup of glass. Derrick grunted and carried on while Jenny swept the floor.

"Mr Thompson," said Jenny.

"Yes?"

"Mr Cartwright still hasn't come down. Should we wake him up?"

"Ah, leave him be, Jenny. After all, the man's eighty-seven."

"Yes, Mr Thompson." She almost went back to her duties, before gathering her courage and speaking up.

"Should we at least send him breakfast?"

"It's alright, Jenny," said Florence. "I'll do it. You can rest when you're done."

"Thank you, Mrs Thompson," she said with a smile as she went back to her business.

Chapter 3

By afternoon, as Jenny was setting the tables, a carriage pulled over, containing several wooden boxes. Sitting next to the coachman was none other than Mr Dawkins. He was of different character, his dialogue direct, his back straightened, his motions steady, and his loose disposition replaced by, in her eyes, the worthy descendant of a lineage of gentlemen.

She flattened herself as he walked through the door, the coachman and his assistant carrying one of the boxes. "Good afternoon, Jenny!" he announced, his boyish energy clashing with the one who stood in his place a few seconds ago.

"Hello, Mr Dawkins," said Jenny, clutching her broom.

"How was your day?"

"Oh, eventful! Very eventful! Yes, second floor," he told the coachman as he handed him his key before turning back to her. "Mr Anderson's wine is simply ecstatic!"

"Yes, but between you and me, don't tell Mr and Mrs Thompson. They're on friendly competition."

"I'll be sure to remember that," he replied before easing her to a shared laugh.

"Oh, you should know," said Jenny, "That there is going to be a party at the mayor's tomorrow night, and you have been invited."

"Oh, that's wonderful! Are you coming?!" Taken aback, she stroked her hair.

"Whether I can or not depends on what Mr and Mrs Thompson wish for."

"I see. But I don't have a suit."

"Mr Thorne's tailor shop is around the corner. I can talk to him if you'd like."

"You did more than you could, Jenny. I am honoured! Now, I apologize for my abruptness, but I need to get back to my luggage."

"Of course." He bid her farewell and returned to applying the last few polishes until she was satisfied.

That night, she ran screaming to Mr and Mrs Thompsons' headquarters. They jumped out of their beds as the door was busted open and she cried "Mr Cartwright's dead!"

Chapter 4

Mr Cartwright remained in his sleeping position; lying on his back, his arms and legs stretched forward. Had Jenny not noticed that his nostrils were still, she wouldn't have realized that something was wrong. Even then, she would have assumed that he died peacefully in his sleep and sent the news in a sorrowful bow. Mr Cartwright was a man with limited time, after all, and he made no qualms about it—but the stains on the bed sheet begged to differ.

His arms, wrists, legs, and neck were all meticulously sliced, with no other signs of aggression throughout the rest of the body. As horrific as it was, Derrick couldn't stop admiring how meticulous and professional it was. The craftsmanship that went into it, where the look on the victim's face didn't even seem to indicate any sign of pain or struggle, suggested that one so conniving and sneaky was somehow able to commit such an action without causing noise or making a mess, was truly astounding.

After they had sent the recovering Jenny to fetch Dr Houseman, he sat at the edge of the bed, the smell already infesting the air. Florence casually leaned against the wall as they quietly glanced at each other.

"It wasn't me," he finally said.

"I know," she said after a moment of silence. "It's not your style." He leaned over the body, going over the marks. By impulse, his hand reached out until it was slapped away by his wife. "That settles it, then. Dawkins did it."

"How do you know that?" he said with a frown.

"Where is he now?"

"What you want me to do? Go bash his brains?"

"Focus," she tapped him on the head and settled both of her hands on his shoulder. "He's probably laughing at us right now."

"How the bloody hell do you know that?"

"Remember Robertson? This is different."

"How so?"

"Blackmail isn't the same as murder, Derrick. Keep a straight head. Watch him closely the next few days. We study his pattern, you go to business as usual, he is challenged, we catch him off-guard, and you off him however you like. Understand?" The blood that leaked through the sheets had started dripping on the floor, the droplet punching the ground, with some of the remains latching onto the tip of Derrick's right slipper.

"Yeah," he mumbled. She backed off as four footsteps came rushing through and Jenny came in with Dr Houseman. He wasn't so much shocked, merely saddened that it had to happen to a man he knew as a friend, especially so late in his life. As a man not yet comfortable with the inevitability of his mortality, this sight was simply another reminder of the ticking of the invisible clock. Still, he couldn't deny that the method of his death was truly strange, for he had never seen it before.

After a quick search, he asked for the coachman that brought him and Jenny to come help him with the body. They will deliver it to the morgue, he explained, and after going through a more thorough examination, will talk to the Chief Inspector about it. As he took his hat, he advised them not to mention this event to anybody until they go public with it.

Jenny was sent home tonight, and halfway through the night, Derrick woke up from a nightmare, but for the life of him, he couldn't remember it. He had another one, and promptly forgot about it as well. He comforted himself by opening the box under his bed. His old friend, the rusty axe, stared back at him. He thanked it, fondling it with sweet words of gratitude, before shoving it back in and going back to bed.

Chapter 5

As a token of gratitude, the axe granted him a soundless sleep. Like a new-born babe, he was pissing, washing, and dressing up before he even realized what he was doing. Florence, who minded her surroundings better than him, adjusted his beard and clothes.

"You look lovely," he said, kneeling himself to her height. She planted a kiss as they went down together.

"About Dawkins, when he comes down, what do we do?"

"Treat him as we always do," she advised him.

"He's going to the party?"

"Possibly. Which reminds me, we'll need to see if your suit fits you."

"I've lost ten pounds, you know."

"Wouldn't hurt to check." They set the tables, and a few minutes later, Jenny stumbled inside. Her back was hunched, her feet were floating, and she could only stare at what laid below her. Her hands were clasped together as if she was in a church, and her eyes were unable to shut. She jumped as she was caught in an embrace by Florence, and found herself silently crying. Embarrassed, Derrick went down to the wine cellar.

"Are you alright, Jenny?" said Florence, her hands on the girl's shoulders. Jenny weakly nodded.

"I-I'm fine, Mrs Florences head hurts, is all."

"You should take the day off."

"No, no!" she insisted, wiping her tears with the edge of her sleeves. "I want to help." *She doesn't want to be alone*, thought Florence.

"Alright," said Florence, "At least sit for a bit and get up when you're ready, alright?"

"Yes, Mrs Florence." As expected, she went into a slumber when she laid her head on the table.

A room from the second floor opened, and audible footsteps were accompanied by the occasional flip of a coin. "Hello there!" said Dawkins as he bent forward and saluted the air.

"Mornin'," said Florence.

"Is Ms Jenny alright?"

"Didn't get enough sleep."

"Ah, she's alright, though, right?"

"I'll let you know when there is trouble." Derrick came out of hiding, with Dawkins finding himself under the watchful gaze of a duo of blank faces.

"Dawkins," said Derrick with a nod.

"Good morning, Mr Thompson!" he replied with a bow.

"I'd like the usual, please."

"The usual, it is. Your equipment arrived?"

"Oh, yes. I hope I haven't created a disturbance."

"We're used to rackets."

"I assure you, rackets here are nothing compared to London!"

"That so?"

"Especially when you are trying to keep a roof above your head."

"Everyone went through that period. Some never get out, if the slums are anything to go by."

"I realize you are blunt, Mr Thompson. But I had no idea you were also cynical," said Dawkins in a chuckle as he flipped his coin.

"Can't afford to be charitable," said Derrick, laying his plate in front of him.

"Ah, thank you."

"Enjoy your meal. By the way, you are invited to be the guest of honour at the mayor's party tonight."

"Yes, Jenny already told me, God bless her. Is Mr

Thorne nearby?"

"Just walk down the street, and when you get to Simone & Simone, turn right. It's the third building after it."

"Thanks."

"Sure." They watched as he munched his food ravenously. Distracted, they scanned for any sign to confirm their suspicions.

When he was done, he paid his dues and flipped another coin. "Well, then," he said, straightening himself,

"It's best to get going. Good day."

"Mr Dawkins," said Derrick as he reached for the door. "What kind of equipment did you bring?" The young man stared at him with a neutral expression he hadn't seen before.

"Surgical tools," he replied in a calm and assuring tone. Derrick's response matched his.

"Oh, alright. Good day."

"Will you both be there?"

"Yeah, I suppose."

"Do you want me to tell Mr Thorne anything?"

"Well," said Florence with a shrug, "Tell him we'll drop by around 3:00, and until then, we'd like to have fitting suits by then."

"Certainly! Bye!"

As soon as he was out of frame, Derrick hurried up and turned his spare key over his room's knob. Heavy cases laid on the desks. They were shut tight, as he couldn't even budge them, hindering his chances of seeing the weapon. An idea hit him and he looked outside, studying the floor and carpet. However, there were no dry bloodstains. He called out to Florence and told her to check the outside of Cartwright's window. She reported back that there were no footsteps in the snow. He then went to Cartwright's room and checked the bathroom, but it seemed untouched. Dizzying about for a minute or two, he groaned in annoyance as he heard the sound of guests coming through.

Chapter 6

Dawkins' left leg was shaking as he made his way down the street. It always happens whenever he disposes of someone. He didn't even want to go outside, but knew that in small towns, the eyes are much more watchful, suspicious, paranoid, and judgmental than any city in the world. Even so, his leg would trigger even when he killed the fellow whose suit he stole in the middle of the road. He never believed that it amounted to guilt, as much as it what he would term a 'tic'; something of great importance to the person is performed, and when the process is done through, excitement combined with stress leaves a small, but noticeable physical act that hangs on for several minutes before being forgotten. He once knew a colleague who, after passing the exams, would constantly twitch his fingers for several days before regaining himself. Suffice to say, he will be fine soon enough. He even chuckled, knowing that the knife hung inside his coat. He complimented himself for the first catch: a former mayor of the town who was rewarded with retirement after his services. A tragedy, but no monumental loss. As he wondered what the atmosphere at the party would be like, he flipped his coin. Heads, as usual.

"Mr Dawkins!" called out someone, and he turned to see Houseman stumbling towards him. For the sake of courtesy, he saved him the energy and walked up to him.

"Hello, good sir!" said Dawkins, shaking his hand. "I don't believe we have been properly introduced."

"No, we haven't. I am Dr Johnathon Houseman, the local doctor."

"Oh, really?! For how long?!"

"Since I came here." The upfront question would have gotten to Houseman, except that he was used to it from every single tourist that passed. "Forgive me for interrupting your daily routine, doctor, but you see, I have been informed that you are a doctor yourself."

"Word travels fast," said Dawkins, feeling the vibration in his leg.

"Yes, for better or worse. Now, I was wondering if perhaps, I could borrow you for a minute. You see, I could use the knowledge of an Oxford graduate."

"Why, certainly! I am all eyes and ears!" The smile seemed to work, for Houseman was encouraged.

"Thank God! Come with me, I'll explain everything. Oh," he said as he paused momentarily before whispering, "Can you keep a secret?"

"Cross my heart and hope to die." Satisfied, they talked in hushes before finding themselves at the local police station. Dawkins couldn't deny an alarming expression, though Houseman mistook it as nervousness and patted him on the back as they went in.

"Hello, Jerry," he said to the officer at the desk, who was doodling a silly face. "This is Dr Dawkins."

Dawkins managed to say, "How do you do?" as his left hand fumbled the coin.

"They're here, sir!" called out Jerry. Isaac and the Chief Inspector, Collins, walked in. Collins was a large man, with square shoulders, a chiselled jaw that was covered by an ageing red beard, and piercing blue eyes. *Wonder how many of Mysore did he shoot*, thought Dawkins as he shook hands with him.

"This way," was the only thing he said as took them to the room where Cartwright's body laid on the table. Dawkins uttered a believable gasp as he observed his marvellous handiwork.

"As you can see, gentlemen," said Collins, "This is a very delicate matter we are dealing with here. A year passes, and here we are again. The bastard's starting again."

"I beg your pardon?" asked Dawkins stupidly, much to the giant's irritation.

"I'm sorry, William, I didn't tell him," explained the apologetic Houseman.

"Convenient," muttered Collins. "A few years ago, doctor, the town was beset by a string of murders. We never figured out how or why it happened; still don't, to be honest. All we knew that was that the victims were random. He, or they, seemed to go after anyone they could get their hands on. When it became clear we weren't going to catch them so easily, the bloke turned into a ghost story, and next thing you know, people would do a song and dance about the Crimson Ox." His breath fumed as he walked back and forth. There was anticipation for a restrained spit before he continued. "Finally, the bastard stopped and we assumed that was the end of that. And now, here he is, at it again. But then Dr Houseman tells me that it's not him."

"Really?" said Dawkins. "A copycat, you mean?" he asked the doctor.

"Well, that's just my hypothesis, but I don't believe that the killer is actually The Cri—culprit." He sunk his head as Dawkins flipped his coin.

"May I see one of the original bodies?" They went down the morgue, and pulled out a middle-aged man's carcass. The display was a mess, its chest sheathed, one leg slashed open, half of his jaw swiped clean, and his back peeled open. Dawkins hated it on sight. Sloppy. Needlessly excessive. Amateur.

"This fellow who was passing by," explained Collins, "Never found any relatives, so we kept him."

"At least he's in good company," said Dawkins, to the amusement of no one other than Houseman.

"Doctors..." grumbled Collins.

"Now, now, inspector. One needs a sense of humour in this business, no matter how twisted it may be. Keeps you a clear head and a running heart."

"Superstition. You die when you are supposed to die."

"Then why bother dealing with this case? By your logic, they died when they are supposed to die, am I correct?"

"Now, now, gentlemen," said Isaac, the first time he has spoken. "There is no need for the antagonism. Let's focus on the case at hand." They agreed with his assessment and went on with the matter at hand.

After an hour of analysis, Dawkins got up and stretched his muscles. "It's not the same."

"Are you certain?" asked an anxious Isaac.

"Yes. For starters, their weapons of choice are different. You said that the others were chopped off in the same manner, correct?"

"Yes," answered Houseman.

"Well then, what you are seeing in the strangers are axe marks. Probably his primary, or only, weapon. Mr Cartwright was killed by an amputation knife. The styles are also different. The Ox certainly lived up to his name. Cartwright's killer was a much more methodical character. I don't believe one would spend a year away just to switch gears, would you?"

They all stood in astonished silence. Collins walked forward and hovered over the bodies; his eyebrows arched. "We're going public with this. Tonight."

"B-but tonight's my arranged..."

"Announce it there, Mr Mayor," said Collins. "We'll tighten security. Keep twenty-four-hour watches. See how he likes it, then." He turned to Dawkins. "I appreciate your help, Doctor, but I want to investigate your luggage."

"Certainly," said Dawkins with a nod.

"Good. Come along. See you tonight, gentlemen." As he followed him outside, Dawkins shook hands with the mayor and the doctor.

"I knew I could count on you, my boy!" said the overjoyed Houseman.

"Don't mention it," said Dawkins as he left.

Collins entered first, explained himself to Florence, and then went up with her permission. He checked the bags, asked a few personal questions, and voiced his annoyance at the sound of the coin's flip. There was no amputee knife to be found, only notes with medical scribbles, some paintings of the human anatomy—Dawkins grinned as he watched staring at the painting of a women, thinking *so he is human, after all*—before ending with his last question:

"You have a reason for coming here of all places, Doctor?"

"I'm on a pilgrimage, sir. A boy making his way through the world."

"That's an awfully dapper suit for somebody on a pilgrimage."

"One has to keep appearances. I'm sure you'd understand." There was another flip before the Inspector sighed and ended the interrogation.

As he went down, he questioned the owners. Florence assured she saw and heard nothing on the night of Cartwright's murder. Derrick wasn't around, so it was onto Jenny. "Did you see Mr Dawkins outside of his room on the night of the murder?" he asked Jenny.

"No, sir."

"Alright, then. Good day."

Dawkins sat watching through his window, then ducked as he saw Collins stumble into view. He waited for twenty minutes until he raised his head again. He was gone.

Probably checking for footprints, he thought as he sighed in relief.

Chapter 7

"Come on, now," mumbled Isaac as he continuously adjusted his tie to no avail. It would always be a matter of time until he called a servant to do it for him.

He faces the mirror and after making sure that everything was set, he decides that it is time. He stood behind the door, shaking as he heard the voices pile over one another. "Jesus," he bitterly drew under his breath before blowing the doors open. They applauded for him; his arms stretched in the air as if trying to hug them all.

The place was bustling with the same old faces, some ageing by the day, others more gracefully. Those who buried their dead, sold food and wine to everyone, the person controlling the candy shop and the tailor somehow had the most graceful shapes in the world.

Some he intentionally avoided as long as he could. Collins was no big deal, seeing as how he would deliberately avoid contact with others. On the other hand, Houseman would never shut up, the Anderson brothers wouldn't stop badgering him about their offer to redecorate his house, and he had to make that bloody announcement about Cartwright. *Why me?* His head demanded.

Collins hated people. No matter how hard he tried to deny it, he couldn't stand their company. It wasn't so much about bowing to pressure of his father's legacy, as much as both of his parents were known for being the first-person, people would go to for a good laugh, or a comforting reassurance, at least before Alzheimer got in their last few years. Of course, as soon as they left, he cut them off, and wouldn't offer them any courtesies. The sentimental ones, he despised them the most. Cartwright also happened to be one of them. Everyone in the crowd looked the same to him, and only his dedication to keep his observation skills sharp would remind him of who's who. Still, they didn't seem to mind, except for Johnathon and George, who still begrudge him for cremating his parents instead of accepting their "services" just because it was a harsh winter that day. He was tapping his foot, waiting for Isaac to get the announcement over and done with so he could go home.

After last night's incident, Jenny didn't feel like coming, but was encouraged to do so by the Thompsons. She looked around, but couldn't find them. Of course, what was she going to tell them in the first place? *How are you Jenny? Oh, just lovely, Mrs Thompson! My headache just got worse, it did!* She accidentally bumped into Thomas, who immediately latched onto her before she repeatedly made her answer clear until he finally gave up. She settled onto a chair and listened to Lisa play the piano as waves of smiles and jeers drifted around her. She thought of poor Mr Cartwright, and was momentarily becoming aware of the structure of the world she lived in, but never really paid much attention to. A quiet night in Sweden, a smallpox outbreak in Milan, both at the same time, on the same day. And here was Mr Cartwright, a new player in this lovely paradox. To Jenny, it was quite depressing, even if a little funny. As to why it was humorous, it was due to how it was, by nature, all out of anybody's hands.

Florence didn't want to come, Derrick much less so, but knew better than to go in hiding in times like these. He wanted to lay low, but she convinced him that they were most likely going to bring up the subject, and may expect to be singled out amongst the crowd.

"Which is why you're going to need to look presentable," she said, giving him a light shave and having Mr Thorne try out a variety of suits until they found one that suited him. She bought herself a suitable outfit that did bring a smile to Derrick's face. In spite of her advancing age, there was a certain beauty to her that he loved. It wasn't glamorous or idealistic: there was some muscle mass certain parts and the flabbiness that comes with growing old in others, but there was a personality backing it up that made others warm to her. If asked, she will simply shrug and say that her labours helped keep her focused and in shape. She greeted Ms Huston first, possibly the closest she'd call a true friend, and they started reminiscence a little bit about the previous ceremonies and all the oddities that came and went.

Derrick had to settle with Mrs Archer, someone even more cynical than him. To make matters worse, Sebastian the Butcher, and the Anderson Brothers would show up and each on would mouth off about their business dealings, as if they were having some wordplay, he was not aware of. If it was, it was easily the most numbing game he ever bore witness to. While they droned on and on, he excused himself, navigated through the crowd, and helped himself to the bouquet, where he poured a glass. He was caught by none other than the man of the hour.

"Spare a dime, will you?" said Isaac, holding out his empty glass. The bottle still in his hand, Derrick observed him before gently bucketing his cup. "Thank you," said his honour, the mayor.

"I hate to admit it," said Derrick, grabbing a bite, "But you've got good taste."

"Thank you," said Isaac, taking one gulp before refiling, "Your pub has nice decorations. Services are really good, too."

"Those were Florence's."

"Oh, really?!"

"Yeah."

"Ah, I see." They stood quiet for several minutes.

"So," said Derrick, "You going to tell me when my payment due is?"

"No, no, no, no, Derrick, let's not go there."

"Really?" said Derrick, raising a mocking eyebrow.

"Look," he said with a sigh, "I've got enough on my plate right now; it can wait. You haven't told anyone, right?"

"No. It's all under wraps."

"Good, good."

"Don't want anyone to hog you?" Isaac raised his eyebrows and massaged his eyes.

"Look. I'm tired, and I've got a headache, ad probably a cold. I'm not in the mood for this."

"Just giving you a taste of your medicine." The mayor swung and faced him in the eye.

"It's not my fault that I'm trying to do my job!"

Derrick glared at him in return and took slow breaths before slowly backing off.

"Fuck you," said Derrick loud enough for both of them and any passers-by to hear. Isaac chuckled, much to Derrick's frustration.

"Just what I'd expect form the likes of you," he said, turning around. Derrick's veins popped, and found his right arm slowly raising the bottle before a shout sent him off-balance and slipped, the wine glass crashing and spraying all over him.

"Hello, everyone!" was the yell that did the trick. Next thing he knew, Dawkins was being attacked by a mob of jeering jokers, yellow teeth and bad breaths, coming from all sides. He kept his cool, however, and played his aloofness to the absolute degree; accidentally tripping over the rug, shaking people with the left hand, and scratching his hair frequently. They dragged him to a nearby chair, and stood in front of him as he talked to them one by one, as if he was Claudius addressing Laertes while the extras looked on.

As he was diving into his history, he spotted the Thompsons slumped in a corner, Florence wiping large spills off of Derrick, Jenny helping them, Collins watching from a corner, and Houseman pacing about, lost in thought.

Then, Isaac called everyone out.

"Ladies and gentlemen," he said, clearing his throat, "Dear friends and family. I am aware that, as much of a novice I could sometimes be, I do genuinely see you all as my true relatives. In fact, I'm glad we're not related, for that makes you all the more special to me." The alcohol was already doing the talking for him, and he was mustering energy so his arms wouldn't flail about. "Which is why—it is necessary to announce—very broken heartedly—Joseph..."

"What?" an impatient customer said.

"JOSEPH DEAD! MR CARTWIRGHT, MR CARTWRIGHT, DEAD! Amputation Knife."

Collins palmed his face as the hall was filled with one or two screams, gasps, and sudden cries from the crowd. He strode up to the centre, pushed Isaac aside, and spoke as loud as he could. "Please, be silent!" The majority were then hushed. "Make no mistake, there is a killer on the loose, and it's not the Crimson Ox." The fear intensified. *Another one?! What are we going to do?! I can't believe it!* Were the expected cries that came out of the crowd.

Collins silenced them all again. "We have already begun investigating the case, and are taking necessary steps to tighten security. You may not have been aware of it, but the guards and servants are being mobilized to guard the house from indoors and outdoors. This type of security will continue until we catch the killer. In the meantime, I ask for your collaboration. As sudden as it all is, I want each and every one of you to contribute to the cause. Please, be our eyes and ears, and help us catch him. I hope you all understand. That is all." He went down the platform and went back to his stationed area. He thought his words mechanical, impassioned, but necessary all the same. He folded his arms and watched.

In a matter of minutes, some guests had already taken their leave. Two hours later, they were all gone, their heads downcast, some angry, others edging on paranoia.

Isaac stood by his own in the middle of the ballroom, and poured himself a drink.

Chapter 8

After escorting Jenny back home, opening their pub, bidding their guests goodnight and goodbye, the Thompsons went back to bathe and put on their bed robes. Florence sat quietly at the edge of the bed, analysing their current situation and how they will make it through the winter, while Derrick was screaming and kicking at the furniture.

"He's taking my spot!" he kept yelling. "He's trying to steal my place! I won't have it! Not me! Bastard's trying to rob me!" He continued circling about until he was exhausted. He collapsed at Florence's feet, tears streaming down his eyes.

"Florence, please! Let me kill someone!" he begged.

Her eyes were pale as she looked down at him. "Is it still there?" she asked in a whisper. He excitedly pulled out the case from under the bag, and showed her the axe. She was firstly taken back at the sight, but soon leaned over and began running her finger through its edges. She handed it back to him. "Go to Emily's tomorrow night and pretend you are getting me some gingerbread. That should give you the edge." He devoutly kissed her hands and then her lips. She planted one in return and combed his hair until he was asleep. When he finally started snoring, she followed him.

Snowfall was heavy this morning, and not many were seen passing, much less entering. Jenny did her best to support and keep their spirits up, but knew it was no use. The rest of the day went on in such fashion until midnight.

All the guests returned early and called it a night, giving Derrick even more time than he could account for. He dressed in his coat, and pulled out his brief case, wiping the dust off of it. He opened the locks, and it sat there, patiently waiting for him.

It was medium sized, with a black edge that looked as sharp as if it was made yesterday. When he bought it that day at the opium den, he found himself imagining what life this relic lead, how many did it chop, and which parts did it favour. It wasn't particularly intimidating, but under the right hands, Derrick knew it could deliver unequivocal fear into the hearts of men. He still remembers the first kill; a bum he had an argument with, one of many in the slums of London. The vibration that crept through his ears, with the blood spraying as the arm went flying and smashing onto a wall was, for Derrick, a sight to behold. That day, he realized that he had found his calling.

He gave it a few swings. He thought he would be rusty, but instead, he felt smooth, agile, and young. He apologized to it for having taken so long. He placed it back in, promising it will be let out soon.

Florence was at the counter when she saw him walk out. She saw his head held up high, a gleam of optimism she had not noticed in him for a long time. His march was different, his boots parading on the ground as he headed towards the door.

"I'm off," he announced, "Will gingerbread be all, dear?"

"Yes, that would be enough," she said in a monotone voice.

"Alright. You need anything Jenny? I'm off to Ms Huston."

"No, no, thank you, sir," said the bewildered Jenny. He bid them farewell, and closed the door before the snow could creep in.

He walked down the empty streets and despite the heavy snow, didn't stop until he reached Emily's front door. He knocked, and walked in, the bell ringing for good measure.

"Oh, Derrick!" exclaimed Emily, a cup of coffee in her hand, her hair slightly ruffled. "Please, come in, come in! What can I do for you?!" She fixed it and composed herself as he approached the counter.

"Sorry for being late," said Derrick.

"No, no, not at all, not at all! How's Florence? Are you two okay?"

"Business was slow today," he admitted. "Hope it doesn't stay that way, though."

"I'm so sorry, Derrick," she said, looking down at her hands, "I wish I could have come today. Tried to help Florence and you."

"Ah, don't think about it."

"I know she likes to do things her way, but that doesn't mean she couldn't use an extra hand," she said sincerely, her heart thumping with every beat.

"That's what I'm here for," he said with a shrug. She blushed and bowed her head again.

"Yes, I suppose you're right. Anyway, what can I do for you?"

"Florence would like some gingerbread." She nodded and smiled as she got to work. He settled the case on the floor, and reached for the lock as she came back with the package. She laid the order on the counter, and he was about to grab the handle, when:

"All done, Ms Huston," came Joseph's voice as he peeked through the corner of the stairs. All three of them froze. Joseph took slow steps downwards before stopping halfway. "Good evening, Mr Thompson," he said with a wave. Derrick nodded in the same movement, and stood up as he looked on in disbelief.

"...Is there anything else you'd like?" said Emily, only her lips moving.

"Some coffee beans," said Derrick numbly. Another package was brought and placed on the counter. He took them, mouthed off a "Thank you," and sluggishly headed towards the door. Every distinctive step, flickering of the flames, and the heavy breathing were as audible as they ever could be. "Look," he said, turning to both of them. "Don't worry. I won't tell." Without waiting for their reply, he opened the door and stood outside.

"Fuck."

Chapter 9

"I see," said Florence as her husband recounted the event, sulked on the edge of the bed with a downcast face. "Well, then, I suppose we should go to bed and think it through tomorrow."

"Yeah," he said as he rolled over to his side. She settled next to him and sighed before turning off the light.

Oliver Dawkins woke up with a headache on the left side of his head. Even when he blinked, it hurt. *Possible dehydration*, he thought as he sleepwalked towards the bathroom. He checked himself in the mirror, but couldn't detect anything wrong. As he filled a bottle of water, he looked outside his window to see two officers engaged in conversation as they passed by.

He waved at them, and they, though surprised, responded with the same gesture.

I wonder how many suspects me, he thought. *Just because Collins came and saw they trust me? Say what you like about the Thompsons, but at least they're not gullible.* He wondered where Jenny stood. He would have found out; except he wasn't targeting her today. Checking his watch, he drank his glass and got dressed. He flipped the coin and it landed on heads. *Success.*

"The room is all yours, Mrs Thompson," he announced as he came down the stairs.

"Off for another walk?" said Florence while Jenny prepared a plate.

"No, actually. I'm off to work."

"Work?"

"Yes! I'm now Dr Houseman's assistant!"

"That was fast."

"Well, you do have to take your steps, right? Otherwise, I wouldn't be able to have more of that wonderful plate of yours."

"I appreciate the compliment. Speaking of which, won't you have breakfast?"

"I'd love to, but I'm running late, to be quite honest. Cheerio!"

"M-Mr Dawkins," called Jenny.

"Yes?"

"Are you alright?"

"What do you mean?"

"Your leg," it was wobbling again. Florence caught a hint of surprise and frustration in the boy's face as he struggled to keep appearance.

"It happens when I'm nervous," he said with a smile.

"Now, I must be off."

"Did I say something wrong?" said an uncertain Jenny.

Florence placed a hand on her shoulder.

"I'll go clean up his room." She left Jenny all alone as the girl served a guest her breakfast.

"She didn't even answer," she said under her breath.

Entering the room, Florence tended to the mattress, and then gave the furniture a good swipe. She ignored the cases, knowing that their owner was smart enough to deduce whether they have been touched or not. She did wonder, however, what other toys did he have in store?

A bell rung and Dr Houseman answered it. "Ah, Dr

Dawkins!" he said, happily shaking the young man's hand at the doorway. "Please, do come in! How are you?"

"I'm fine, thank you. I hope I'm not late!" He pulled a bashful smile as he quickly scanned the building. It was one of the smallest places in town, a senile place clearly reserved for one occupant. Like most doctors' houses, it was a depressing affair. He took his first step through and could feel every crack of the wooden floor.

"Quite a party, wasn't it?" said Dawkins, fighting the impulse to tear the place down.

"Oh, yes—quite," said the old man, bending his head downwards in embarrassment. "Well, now, my office is this way." As they moved towards the staircase, something caught Dawkins' eye. This was the first place he had visited to be populated with books. The living room, which was the first place one entered, had a shelf of books, outlined in alphabetical order in front of a cosy chair placed besides the fireplace. He couldn't read all of the titles, but he did scan a mixture of medical essays as well as some fictional prose, possibly for entertainment purposes.

"You've got quite the collection, Doctor," said Dawkins as they went upstairs.

"Well, someone has to do something in their spare time."

"Quite true. I suppose this town doesn't have much patience for literature."

"Oh, they do love stories as much as anyone else, but everyone has their own diversions, that's all. Almost forgot! Forgive my rudeness, but would you like some tea?"

"Coffee will do." He didn't have any, so tea it was.

They had to go back down and Dawkins was requested to sit in the dining room while he came back. The kitchen, like the rest of this house, was small and claustrophobic, the dining room only slightly less so.

There were no pictures of relatives, nor even of himself. As he watched the old man from the distance, Dawkins felt as if he was watching a puppet theatre.

They discussed a variety of subjects during their discussion, be it their past, London, the politics, what practices and terminologies will prevail, which will be abandoned, and so one and so forth. By impulse, Dawkins would take out and flip his coin, and was eventually long enough for the doctor to take notice.

"May I ask what that's about?"

"This is my good luck charm." The doctor laughed.

"Really? I never thought you'd be the type to believe in such things."

"I can show if you'd like. Heads or tails?"

"Tails." It landed on heads.

"Only a dog follows its tail," said Dawkins as he kneeled back in victory. Houseman sat in silence before proposing that they visit his office.

After a tour in another part of his dollhouse, they prepared their equipment in preparation for today's workload. An hour later, patients had arrived.

Although he regarded him as a pitiful man, Dawkins couldn't help but admit that the doctor was a professional and was able to keep a lively and optimistic chatter with his guests. He kept going until five p.m., when the last one arrived. It was none other than the mayor himself, complaining from stomach and muscles aches. Checking him, Houseman warned him that he had been consuming too much alcohol and should be more physically active. "Get yourself together, now!" said a concerned Houseman, with the mayor only coughing in response, his eyes beady and his mood miserable. "I'll have Dawkins call your guard so."

"I'm alone," said Isaac in a low voice.

"What?"

"I came alone! I-I didn't want anyone to see me."

"You can't go around doing that, not when there's a killer out there! Besides, how are you going to leave now?"

"I'll take him," said Dawkins, volunteering.

"Are you sure?" asked Isaac.

"Certainly, sir. Can't have you on your own in the dark, can we?"

"I suppose so. Alright." They held onto each other shoulder to shoulder and were on their merry way.

Dawkins waved goodbye to Houseman before the door was closed.

Chapter 10

"Can't stand that place," uttered Isaac, "Bloody hospital of a house is all cramped and stuffy. Feels like a tomb."

"Well, Houseman is pretty old," said Dawkins, looking about for the presence of guards, "So, he probably sees no point in changing things."

"At least have some dignity to be courteous, damn it!"

The man tripped and slammed headfirst into the snow. He sat up and coughed endlessly.

"It was rather stupid of you to do this," said Dawkins, "All because you were scared of what people were going to say about you." He spotted the arrow that showcased directions and directed him towards home.

Halfway through the journey, there is a bridge with a river bank underneath.

"I did it once, and it slapped it me in the face."

"Really?"

"My mother was a school teacher. My father was a lawyer. He represented Cartwright. When he came up with the idea for this place, they were there from the beginning. You get it?! My family built this town!"

"Sorry..."

"No problem."

"I entered law school. Cartwright probably saw something in me, and next thing you know, I'm going to be the mayor of this place. I wanted to share this moment with someone—it was Florence."

"You caught my interest!"

"Thought so," said the mayor bitterly. "I was more than ready to tell her. I did, actually. But my parents couldn't take it. Not an innkeeper's daughter, they said! She knew, of course. I told them if I wasn't going to have her, then I'll have no one. You could imagine how well they took it, the old fools. Then, next thing you know, some bloke from the outside comes in and settles, and of all people, Florence picks him!"

"So, Derrick isn't from here?"

"No. Never knew his deal."

"I see. Well, here we are." He stopped at the entrance of the bridge. "Home, sweet home. Have a lovely night, Isaac."

"You too. You're more than welcome. You're part of the family, after all." He took a few steps forward, and didn't realize until it was too late that he was drooling blood. Losing his balance, Isaac tipped off the edge and took a dive.

"You old fool," said Dawkins. He watched the body swim away before sinking, then took a walk around another part of town to mark his footsteps, and finally put on a frightened face as he ran screaming for help.

Chapter 11

The news of Isaac's death spread across town, and there was a period of panic and anger in the upcoming days. Collins had to deal with the barrage of people demanding how exactly they expect to be protected when his honour, the mayor, was already a shambling corpse. George and Johnathon were anxiously waiting for the report, neither of the two comfortable with the ordeal. Derrick contemplated barging into Dawkins' room and killing him, but Florence would hold him back and ask him to be patient. When guests dined at their headquarters, the atmosphere was dead quiet.

As for Oliver Dawkins, he explained how he helped walk Isaac to the entrance of the bridge, where the man ordered him to let go. He obliged and left, taking a well-known short cut back to the Thompsons', when he saw his body drifting. Houseman attesting Dawkins' presence with him gave Collins no reason to believe that he was particularly guilty, but in either case, he demanded to see the surgical tools again. The young doctor complied, having brought them to work. An amputation knife laid among them, freshly bought, gleaming among the veteran tools. It was paid on Houseman's wallet, from the marketplace outside the borders of the town.

Asking for any clues, Dawkins informed them that the victim died from a stab in the neck by a small Dominion butcher knife.

"Butcher knife?" said Collins, raising his eyebrow. He glanced at it and saw a hand sized knife draped in blood, held by a dull red handle.

"Yes, butcher knife it is," declared Dawkins.

"Who would wait outside the snow with a butcher knife for God knows how many hours to kill someone?"

"The Crimson Ox?" suggested Houseman.

"No. Like Dawkins said, he only used an axe that was how every murder went. It's got to be the other one."

"Are you sure? What makes you think the Ox wouldn't change strategies? He's been quiet for so long, hasn't he?"

"You are right, but even if this was his comeback, he wouldn't go easy on the mayor. Remember Cartwright? "Isaac is the same; apart from the stab wound, the body was left alone. It's the other one, it's got to be."

Dawkins wiped his glasses and stroked his chin as he considered the chief inspector's explanation.

"So, he's of the varied type," said Dawkins.

"Right."

"A trickster," murmured Houseman. "If the Crimson Ox was hard to find, this one would be trouble."

"Yeah." Collins played with his beard, well aware that as suspicious as he was, he didn't have any backed evidence to prosecute Dawkins.

"By the way, Doctor," said Dawkins as the inspector took his leave, "What should we call him?"

"Don't!" belted out Collins as he slammed the door shut.

He decided to do another overall check around town. The officers had nothing to offer from their posts, so he started squeezing people, but found out that they were quite honest about the fact that they stayed inside their houses after leaving the party.

"Just like you told us to," said Mrs Archer with a stiff lip. He ignored her and moved on with the routine before reaching Sebastian's doorstep.

"Hello, Sebastian," said Collins, catching the sound of blood draining the sewage.

"Ah, detective!" said the sweating butcher, his apron decorated like a canvas. "Please, come in, come in." This was the second time the stench of naked meat reached his nostrils, causing him to cover his nose in quick seconds before the owner turned his head. "I've heard about the mayor," said Sebastian, offering him a clean chair, "Very awful. But don't fret yourself over it."

"That's not what the others have been saying."

"Ah, forget about them. They're in panic, that's all."

"You're surprisingly optimistic."

"I keep my chin up, just like mother taught me," said Sebastian as he shrugged his shoulders.

"You wouldn't mind if I ask some questions, would you?"

"Of course not!"

"Dr Houseman and his associate found that the murder weapon constituted of a small Dominion butcher knife.

Tell me, Sebastian, what does yours look like?"

Sebastian's eyes gleamed, but he kept himself composed.

"Well, I have several Dominions, and one of them is a small one with a red handle."

"Is it sharp?" The Butcher laughed heartily, and stopped when he realized the inspector wasn't sharing his sentiment. He coughed and admitted that it was. Collins asked to see it, but when they opened the cupboard, it was gone. The barber excused himself and searched for it in other areas, Collins calmly watching as the sweating figure was ever so slowly dancing about more and more frantically. As he passed by him, he grabbed the shoulder and pulled him to the ground, bumping into one of the cow carcasses along the way.

"Inspector, I know what you think, but I swear I didn't kill anyone!" said Sebastian as he got on his knees amidst pained groans. "You know me better than that!"

"I only know any of you by association," said Collins as he made the way for his men to grab and take him away.

That night, George and Johnathon were playing cards while sharing a bottle of wine. Naturally, George won as Johnathon's mind was already plagued with liquor. He stumbled off his chair, throwing the usual mumbled vitriol at the older man while he leaned against his bed.

"...what?" said Johnathon.

"I said," said George, putting the cards back in place, "That we'd better look over the preparations once again. Please don't give me that look. It's a big day tomorrow, and if it goes well, we'll survive under this roof throughout winter."

"What's the difference?" said George, saliva leaking through his mouth, "There'll be others."

"Is that the reason you pray to each night before bed?"

"You're still here?"

“Let’s hope so, for your sake.” Defeated, Johnathon said no more. “If you just sober up,” said George as he helped him up, “You’ll do fine.”

“My daughter,” said Johnathon, “Didn’t even write after the wedding. Not even a scrap of a bottle. Bitch.”

“Sometimes I felt like kicking you out,” said George as he sat on the bedside chair. “Get some rest,” He advised, drawing the blankets.

George tried to sleep, but no such luck came. His insomnia, ever so present, wouldn’t let his troubled mind be. It was partly due to the usual grievances that plague an old man’s mind; the passing of time, the dichotomy between acceptance and fear of death, the questioning of whether he had accomplished enough in his life, and flights of imagination he couldn’t stop indulging in. Partly it was due to the main reason Johnathon was even more drunk than usual: the killings. They bring food to the table, certainly, but still—he remembered asking an executioner how he coped, and the man replied, “I pray every night that I become a bogeyman, so that the smart ones would think twice about it.”

He ignored the sounds, brushing it off as the rush of the wind. But the more he listened, the more he realized how distorted it was. His suspicions were conformed when a distant glint of orange invaded the walls. He opened the door, and stood in horror.

Someone was being set on fire.

Chapter 12

Collins was stampeding down the streets in his bed robes as his uniform hung onto his shoulders for dear life in the blizzard. It wasn't hard to find the scene of the crime, with the smoke in the sky practically dancing naked. Despite the breeze, the townspeople were all there, with Sebastian's charred corpse front and centre, crucified beyond redemption.

"What the hell happened?" his demands were met with numb looks from the crowd, until a bruised guard approached and explained that the townspeople rioted and broke into prison, dragged Sebastian and did this to him.

The sight didn't necessarily shock Collins, he had stopped vomiting by then—but the complacency of the crowd, the gap in his head that made him think how these people broke in, dragged their neighbour, and got rid of him beyond any doubt, that horrified him. He had them forcefully removed, and after a long banter among the groups, some claiming whose brilliant idea it was, they were shoved into their houses. His thoughts scrambled about, knowing that his men were awaiting their orders. He belted them, demanding to know why they couldn't stop the commotion. The timid fellow reminded him that they were advised not to use brute force. They didn't know any better.

Somehow, he found himself back in his room, still drenched in his uniform. His forehead was oiled in sweat, with his hair crumbled about. He sleepwalked to the bathroom and stared at the mirror, surprised at the haggard eyes, the creature in front of him bore. He stumbled out of fright, the moon being the only bearable thing he can lay eyes on at the moment. He spotted pieces of ash on his shoulders, and immediately opened the window and began wiping them off. He watched the smoke disintegrate, fractures of it remaining as his men went to work, presumably under his orders. He slumped into bed, asking Sebastian for forgiveness as tears streamed down his face.

Watching the festival from an unoccupied room's window, Dawkins flipped his coin once again. Landing on tails, he sighed and stuffed it back. In some fashion, the witch hunt was quite a shock, even to him. Yet, he wouldn't have necessarily expected anything less from the likes of them. The fact that they fell for it as soon as possible was what amused him. At least with the others, it would take some time before someone starts the revolution. *I wonder who started it*, he thought, when something caught him off the corner of his eye.

The figures of Emily and Joseph were slipping off to her shop. Two possibilities arose; they were either off to a good shagging, or they were planning to escape. He considered, and went for another toss; tails. *Oh well*, he decided, *I can settle for better.*

"Is this it?" asked Joseph, holding a notebook. Emily nodded in reply, snatching it as she shoved it into her backpack. The case was stuffed already, and she impatiently considered and threw off things they didn't need. For his part, Joseph packed some of her supplies—coffee beans, homemade ingredients, and other supplies for the business, while he only took his collection of seashells.

"Alright, let's go," she said, grabbing the keys.

"Are you sure?" said an uncertain Joseph.

"I may be passionate, but never sentimental," she said, holding his hand. He bowed his head and nodded.

"You're right. Come on, Thomas is waiting." She bid her life's work goodbye, sent her blessings to Florence and Mrs Baker, and they were off.

They reached at the outskirts, with Thomas waiting with a carriage under a tree. He helped lay their equipment and embraced his friend before watching them ride off.

The next day, their bodies were found on the side of the road, chopped to bits. Even the horses were not spared from the ordeal.

Chapter 13

"Oh, Lord, have mercy!" cried Houseman as he slumped onto his chair. The man hated being overworked and wouldn't even give it a thought in his current age. Therefore, when Dawkins offered to dissect the bodies without his input, the veteran gladly shut his eyes and snoozed off.

Two hours later, he was nudged awake by Dawkins, who asked him to come along. Much to his misfortune, Collins was there. "How can I help you, gentlemen?" he stupidly asked.

"You said you wanted to say something," said Collins to Dawkins. He highlighted the corpses, which prompted a look of frozen terror from the sight.

"Gentlemen," said Dawkins, "Your old friend has resurfaced." Silence enveloped the room, an element of surprise present in the trio.

Collins, no matter how hard he tried, showcased an expression of distraught horror, and Houseman almost fainted. Dawkins drew a neutral stance, and pretended to be studying the bodies, when in fact, he wanted to do nothing more than jump in joy. He was proud, shaking the invisible hand of a new rival with genuine respect. *But certainly, to showcase such admiration in public would seem queer*, his rationality thought, so he stood in silence as the duo fettered about in shock.

"Do you realize what this means?!" said Houseman, wiping his wax forehead. Collins stared at the ground before responding:

"We've got two of them."

"Oh, dear God..."

"Quiet, Houseman!" snapped Collins. "Your whining won't help much. Listen to me," he addressed both of them, "as far as anybody knows, Emily and Joseph disappeared. Hell, some of them are probably assuming that one of them was the killer. So, here's what we'll do; we stay quiet about this. Keep the people off guard. Otherwise, we'll have a repeat of yesterday."

"But how are we going to catch them?" asked Houseman.

"I've already notified that suspicious activities are to be reported to me. This'll keep them busy, so I'll let them spy on one another."

"Unwitting allies—clever!" said a delighted Dawkins.

This bastard is more manipulative than I thought, he thought.

"Exactly. Any questions?" They didn't respond. He took it as silent agreement and bid them farewell.

"Quite a crowd," said Dawkins, "Spying on one another, dishing out secrets, even at the cost of death. And here I was thinking it was any different from London." The old doctor's sad face was still as he wrapped the bodies.

"It was always there, Dawkins," said Houseman, "It was just slow this time of the year."

"I suppose. Good night, sir." He didn't hear a reply as he left. He flipped the coin once again; heads. A merry laughter erupted from his heart.

Chapter 14

Derrick and Florence had a fight last night. It wasn't because he murdered Emily and Joseph, mind you, as much as he didn't ask for her permission first. True, she did allow him to go after her that night, but when he came back to tell her of his failure, she suggested that they wait and consider what to do next. But when he saw them hurrying away to the outskirts of town, clearly setting off on the road, he retorted to her it was a now or never situation. The Crimson Ox has finally returned! His grandiose appraisal of himself got on her bad side, and her contempt brought him down a notch.

Of course, Jenny simply assumed they had one of those usual harmless squabbles between spouses. Still, she was never comfortable around such fights; aside from the rising tension and the loudness of the participants' shouts, the experience itself was one she wouldn't want to go through again, with her forced to become the audience member to her mother and father's arguments, no matter how hard she tried to retreat in her head. She couldn't even take care of herself, as she would do things she would rather forget, just to get away from the noise. She ate even when she wasn't hungry. She indulged in carnal desires, and would enact imagining herself in situations that were physically and mentally humiliating. She would sit in her room all day, at some point even skipping her job, until Florence lost her temper and warned that she will replace her. Eventually, she broke down and confessed, and after hearing her story, much to her surprise, Derrick gave her enough encouragement to patch herself up and even taught her several techniques of mental coping. She would like to say that she is half way through, even if elements that reminded her of the past would still intimidate her.

Her thoughts were interrupted when several guests came in for dinner. After the events regarding Sebastian, the atmosphere had lowered. If people talk, it's only in close groups, only with those they really trusted.

When Dawkins entered, he was the first one to try to speak plainly to others. They shrugged it off as him being new.

"The usual?" said Derrick as the young man walked up to him. His mood was softer, the smell of his arms hair awash with fresh shampoo.

"No, thank you, Mr Thompson, I'm off to bed."

"Sweet dreams, then."

"Why, thank you! By the way, has anyone seen Miss Emily? I was hoping to buy some coffee beans, but the shop is closed." Derrick kept a blank face as he responded.

"No, I haven't. Florence?"

"Well, she hasn't told me," said Florence in the voice of a bewildered and worried friend who was nonetheless too occupied to give her full attention.

"I see. Oh, well, good night."

"Good night."

Chapter 15

"So, how did it feel?" Florence asked her husband in time for bed. She saw a smile curve across his mouth, humbled by some degree of bashful shyness.

"Well," he began, trying to come up with the right words, "It felt—ah, what was it?!"

"Refreshing? Elating?"

"Yes, yes! Elating—it couldn't have come at a better time! I am ready, Florence! Ready to go out again and show the bastards…"

"Derrick."

"Yes?"

"They don't know." He gasped in silence. His head flashed to today's prior events. Slowly, the cracks started to show. No one whispered Emily or Joseph's names. No one was, in fact, barely discussing it. No one was thinking about it. No one knew.

She patiently waited as he thrashed and stomped about the room, until he collapsed in the corner to catch his breath.

He stood up, hunched over with a determined grimace. He pulled the suitcase and grabbed his coat and the axe. "I'm going out."

“Suit yourself,” she said with a shrug. As he headed for the door, he stopped put a gentle hand on her shoulder.

“We’ll talk about this when I get back, okay?” he whispered. She gave him a blank expression that betrayed no emotion, and he stumbled through the door in embarrassment.

“Use the back,” she said, and he came back, pushed the wardrobe aside, and crawled through a crack big enough for a man of his size.

He got off the opening, and found a guard standing with his back turned to him, stretching his neck. He lent him a hand, and gave his head some smacking for good measure before decorating and throwing the body in a convenient location for other posts to spot.

That night, the section of the town where the primary murder occurred was near the bridge that led to the deceased mayor’s land. Should one get off, they would pass by Mrs Archer’s bakery and the tailor house. There would be no reason to be afraid, considering that the freezing weather sent everybody home locking their doors and windows, and two guards were standing over a good view of the town.

Unfortunately, the duo that day were off on private businesses. One was so drunk he could barely stand and the other was frolicking with one of the office’s chamber maids. Archer was the first to notice the body that sprawled on the ground, a mixture of white, red, blonde, and a green hood all cobbled together in the last minute.

Underneath the hood was a face he recognized. It belonged to Jenny.

Chapter 16

Dawkins woke up in the middle of the night thanks to the continuous shouting outside. A*nother lynching?* He mumbled in annoyance as he forced himself upwards. He opened the window as some of the children ran by.

"Hey!" he called out to them, "What's going on?!"

"Jenny's dead!" He froze as they ran off. Getting dressed, he ran to the site and made his way through. The body, like Emily and Joseph, was haphazardly chopped out of proportions, without a sense of delicacy. Now, if she died by his hands, he would have treated her with more respect. *What a waste,* thought Dawkins.

"Is that the Crimson Ox?" he asked with a fake tone tinged with genuine curiosity. The crowd was quiet for a minute, and slowly backed away from him and the body as if they were both diseased.

Then one of the children yelled about the dead guard, and he rushed over there like everyone else. The poor bastard was pretty much beyond repair, with a decapitated head and all. Dawkins looked around, and saw that some were still in their houses. Mr and Mrs Thompson happened to be among the crowd, with the latter burying her face in her husband's shoulder while he comforted her. The figure of Collins had arrived just now.

When he got in earshot of the crowd, the words "Chopped," "Crimson Ox," and other spells of doom were already spreading. The inspector quickly dispatched the scene, giving his men license to violently push them back. Some didn't appreciate the gestures, and a small riot erupted. It was thankfully controllable, considering that most of the citizens were already well into their final years, and savagery was their natural inclination, not violence. The next day, he held a town meeting, and the results were chaotic. Some begged to have an inspection from outside, preferably from the Scotland Yard, others rebuked, claiming it will spread unwanted rumours and keep potential customers and business dealings away. Some demanded that they be given weapons for self-defence, and around three hours in, they started accusing one another of being the murderer. The entire process was a waste of time, and by the end of the meeting, he ordered them all out, and lumped his head on the desk with his hands resting on the back of his head.

Mrs Archer has witnessed death before. The concept was old to her since the death of her twin sister. Yet, whenever she tried to shake hands with it whenever it passed by, she would never truly gain the courage to do so. It wasn't because she didn't want to die; she has accepted that notion long ago, but it was the executions themselves, the methods that, no matter how simple it was, could lead to death, and even worse, more devices were increasing the more time passed. When even the act of eating could lead to death, it became hard for one to appreciate the basics of life.

George and Johnathon got their burial plans ready as they consulted with the parents of the respective victims. The conversations themselves were straightforward—a proper burial, nothing more and nothing less—but watching people shake and tear up so openly, as if they have been waiting for an excuse to do it, drove them, especially Johnathon, who would bury his hands between his knees whenever his fists would clench. He was still on good terms with the bottle, but only felt numbness as of now. And possibly envy as well, if only for how George managed to keep himself composed in spite of everything, going on with business as usual.

But George sensed, no, he knew, that this wasn't the end. Others were coming, and he wouldn't be surprised if the killer would be gunning for them.

The Thompsons spent the night at Jenny's parents, doing their best to elevate Jenny's passing, letting them know that she was a dedicated worker and a dear girl. It was useless, of course, but one ought to try their best in situations like these. Obviously, Florence did all the talking, with Derrick disguising his silence as a show of respect to the corpse he mangled.

He wanted to get out of there, to celebrate. His impatience wore thin when the father, in disbelief, whimpered how he was still around, after all. *Of course, I was, you fuckin' idiot!* Derrick wanted to shout, but what could he do? And the scene with the crowd, with Dawkins there to boot! Rubbing it in his face like that, it was no doubt a glorious moment for him! No doubt about it; the Crimson ox has returned.

Three days later, Dr Houseman died of a heart attack.

Chapter 17

In hindsight, Houseman was the most important person in this town. Like a passing king whose subjects have no one to follow, his funeral shook his patients and neighbours. With no doctor to relay their problems to, many have decided to pack and leave. There was nothing in particular against Dawkins, but like most successors, most lacked the patience to wait for improving results concerning such delicate matters; he didn't take it personally, of course. Besides, should he optimize the classic strategy—people come to doctor's office, and are last seen there, never to return—would arise suspicion.

Only a handful of soldiers remained with Collins. The young ones left with their families, and the ones that remained were old or had nowhere to go. He dismissed them, locked himself in his house, and never showed his face again. Only Johnathon and George paid him a visit, letting him know where they are planning to open their new business, and wished him well, should he ever consider reliable caretakers when the time came.

The Thompsons, along with only a tiny handful of people stayed, but it didn't matter. They knew that Derrick had triumphed, that this place will be a ghost story, and he will be its beating heart. The Crimson Ox now stands among the legends.

All what's left is to clean up some of the remains.

They were seated at the counter at midnight, the motel empty and silent, except for the opening of a door, and incoming footsteps from the second floor, followed by a flip of a coin.

"I won," said Derrick as Dawkins came into view. The Oxford graduate didn't take offence as he flipped a chair and sat down.

"I confess," said Dawkins, "Hearing about it and seeing them offer you different perspectives. I admire your handiwork. Vulgar, but clearly passionate. You owe me a thank you. Without me, you would have stayed a slob."

"Why did you come here?" said Florence. "What was your plan?"

"Nothing. I simply hear these funny little stories about certain folks that walk among their fellow men, with desires and methods that are—unfavourable to the public conscious. So, I pay them a visit, and see whether they are as good as they say."

"So, you kill people just to satisfy your curiosity," said a restrained Florence.

"Now, now, Mrs Thompson. No need to come to Jesus right now. I have enough of that on Sunday." They sat in silence as he quietly flipped the coin, if only out of habit.

"Am I good enough for you?" Florence looked at her husband, his voice tinged with curiosity and anticipation.

"Like I said," said Dawkins, "I respect your handiwork."

"Well, I appreciate it," said Derrick as he brandished the axe from underneath the counter, "But I'm not done yet."

"Neither am I," replied Dawkins. "Collins is waiting for me."

"Collins?" the pair said in confusion. The coin landed on heads.

"You see, while you two were too busy melting each other's tits, I was spying on our mutual friend. He's gone insane, I tell you. Target practicing."

"What are you talking about?" said Florence.

"He's going to knock on every door and shoot the remaining citizens, including me and you. Now, how would you feel about that, Mr Thompson? A third lunatic entering the foray, only, when you really think about it, that wouldn't be highly recommendable, would it? He shoots you, then me, then the rest of this population, and when news spread, perhaps, after all these years, it would make sense why you were never caught. Because the local chief inspector, Detective Collins, the man, the myth, the legend, was the Crimson Ox!"

Chapter 18

Years later, the story of the Crimson Ox would be told as a ghost story in one way or another. It would be told as a lullaby, as an actual case investigated by historians, be turned into a subject of parodies that diminish the original meaning, or turned into a term to be utilized against one's scapegoat enemies. In either case, Derrick would accept all of such conditions as long as it was, he who received such appraisal and derision. He worked too hard for it to be gone, he risked his wife's life for it, and no matter who or what stood in his way, and he was not going to lose it now.

He was in a rush, the cold, the houses, their occupants, and the whirl of the wind were but invisible glimpses that he paid no heed to. All he saw was what stood in front of him; a house, and the man who lived there.

He went with a surprise attack, barging through the window, a great brown bear. The bulb that lit the room crashed and Collins shot at the darkness. The silhouette of the intruder shifted about with remarkable speed, and although his second shot was better, the rustiness of time reared its ugly head at the wrong time. As he contemplated bringing out his old friend, Collins once vowed to never shoot another person. He kept his word.

Dawkins and Florence were having a drink as they waited for the Crimson Ox to deliver the news. He breathed a sigh of relief as he saw a familiar giant barge through the door, drenched in blood and guts.

On the contrary, Florence looked pristine as ever. In fact, in his eyes, she never looked more beautiful. Even as a corpse, he knew why he loved her.

"Artificial leech," said Dawkins as he pointed to the device that sat between them. A thin box with protruding knives with rotating knives soaked in blood sat there, its traces not far behind, starting from Florence's shoulder. "I didn't want her to suffer. I can't believe it myself but I'm fond of you two. Come along and sit next to her; I want to give you a respectful death."

Derrick slowly recovered and mechanically sat next to his wife. The axe, gripped tight in his hand, was gently placed on the table. "Would you like to hear a story?"

"Certainly," replied Dawkins.

"I was born in London like you. Didn't go to Oxford, though. I belonged to the slums. Compared to others, I got off easy. Eighteen, I was, when I did it. A bum wanted my coins. Told him no, started raising his voice. Shut him up. Thought it was self-defence at first, but got the picture later on. Landlord came in, threatened to pull me out. Knew I had to leave soon, anyway. He could have waited. Had a late night, had to wake up for work early the next day. Drunk bloke wouldn't stop singing. Looked and sounded the same as the first one, made me uncomfortable. Young lady lived a floor above. Owned a flower shop, minded her own business. Got rid of her too. Kept some of the flowers for myself. Mistake, it was. Had to flee, getting whoever, I could along the way.

Got here, of all places, and got a job under this roof. Florence was the only one. Houseman, Archer, the caretakers, Isaac—walking abortions, they were! Confessed. Taught me to be more careful. Showed me how to make a living. Allowed me to talk to others without embarrassment. Gave me a reason to be happy."

"So, on her behalf, I propose a deal." Dawkins leaned over in interest.

"Go on."

"Heads, you kill me. Tails, I kill you." A mutual smile of agreement was on their faces. The coin was flipped. There was a rough *thud* as it landed on the palm.

Tails.

The End

CPSIA information can be obtained
at www.ICGtesting.com
Printed in the USA
BVHW040743130423
662286BV00016B/975